Invitations to Personal Reading
Curriculum Foundation Classroom Library
Scott, Foresman and Company

3rd Grade

Realistic Stories	
Beanie	Ruth and Latrobe Carroll
Blaze Finds the Trail	C. W. Anderson
Eddie and Gardenia	Carolyn Haywood
Nappy Has a New Friend	Inez Hogan
Pierre Pidgeon	Lee Kingman

Biography and Historical Fiction	
Clara Barton: Soldier of Mercy	Mary C. Rose
Daniel Boone, Boy Hunter	Augusta Stevenson
The First Year	Enid Meadowcroft
Martin and Abraham Lincoln	Catherine C. Coblentz
Susannah, the Pioneer Cow	Miriam Mason

Fun and Fancy	
Favorite Fairy Tales Told in France	retold by Virginia Haviland
How Big Is a Foot?	Rolf Myller
How Space Rockets Began	Le Grand
The Man, the Boy, and the Donkey	retold by Katherine Evans
The Traveling Musicians	Grimm Brothers

Books Too Good to Miss	
Famous Paintings	Alice Chase
The Golden Touch	Nathaniel Hawthorne
Looking-for-Something	Ann Nolan Clark
Nibble, Nibble (poems)	Margaret Wise Brown
Wee Gillis	Munro Leaf

Books to Enrich the Content Fields	
Discovering Dinosaurs	Glenn Blough
The Hole in the Tree	Jean George
Little Sioux Girl	Lois Lenski
True Book of Space	Illa Podendorf
Your Body and You	Alice Hinshaw

LITTLE SIOUX GIRL

ROUNDABOUT AMERICA

Come, let us look at the ways of life
in our country. Let us go into out-of-the-way
corners, up on the hills and down in the
valleys, into city streets and village homes.
Let us see and get to know the people.
Here and there, round about America, are
friends worth knowing.

The *Roundabout America* stories
are vivid scenes from real life,
in short-story or longer form,
for younger readers.

LITTLE
SIOUX GIRL

Written and Illustrated by
Lois Lenski

J. B. Lippincott Company
Philadelphia, 1958

Special Scott, Foresman and Company Edition
for the *Invitations to Personal Reading* Program

This edition is printed and distributed by
Scott, Foresman and Company by special
arrangement with J. B. Lippincott Company, East
Washington Square, Philadelphia, Pennsylvania 19105.

Foreword

A tiny village on a plateau by a river bank—a church, a school, a house for the teacher and a dozen log cabins. That was all. It was in the Standing Rock Indian reservation in the Dakotas, and here Sioux Indian children lived.

Wind and dust and hot sun were their daily companions. Cut off from the world by a rough, at times impassable road, they ran and played and were happy. I visited them in 1950, talked to them and loved them.

Since then, the school has been closed, the Indian families have moved away and the cabins are empty.

But here is their story.

Lois Lenski

My thanks to Mary Van Danacker, their valiant teacher, to Ruth Carter, Ruby Hetterle and other South Dakota friends for their generous help.

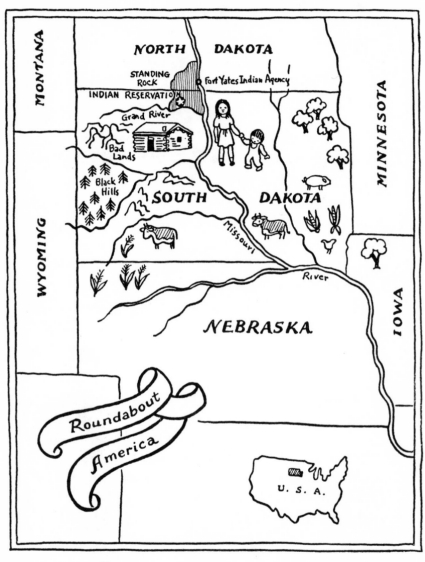

Location of Story

Contents

Chapter 1

A WARM HOUSE

"Is winter coming?" asked the little girl.

"Look at the dark sky," said her mother. "Those clouds are full of snow."

The little girl buttoned her sweater tightly. A chilly wind blew across the prairie.

"I like summer better," said Eva. "I like to go swimming in the river."

Her mother laughed.

"Now you go to school every day," she said.

"Now you learn to read in a book. Now you do what teacher tells you to. No more can you swim, pick berries and ride horseback over the prairie ... No, not for many moons."

Mrs. White Bird brought a pail of warm water from the log cabin. A hole had been dug in the ground at the side of the house, with loose dirt left in it. She poured the water into the hole, and with a stout stick, mixed the dirt into mud. Several dogs played nearby, barking noisily.

"Watch out, baby!" called the woman. "Eva, come take your little brother away."

A small boy of two toddled toward the mud hole, ready to tumble in. Eva pulled him back.

"No, no, Joel," she said. "Stay away from the mud."

She turned to her mother. "Will it be a cold winter?" she asked.

"The cattle are going to starve, the old man says," said her mother. "There will be four feet of snow."

"How does Uncle Nick know?" asked Eva.

"Because the geese are flying low," said Mrs. White Bird, "and the cornhusks are thick. That means a hard winter. Nicholas One Elk has lived over ninety winters on the prairies. Uncle Nick is a man of wisdom—he knows."

Eva White Bird was a little Sioux girl. She lived in the town of Black Horse, high on a plateau in the Bad Lands of Dakota, on a government Indian reservation. The town was divided by a small creek which flowed into the Grand River. A rough winding road came from over the rocky hills and followed along the creek. On one side stood the little white church and the

school, and scattered about were a dozen log cabins. A bridge of logs crossed the stream.

Off in the distance on all sides, jagged masses of cliffs and hills rose up. Above all was the great bowl of the sky, filled now with dark threatening clouds.

"Come and help, my daughter," said Mrs. White Bird. "We must get the house ready for winter."

The woman took up mud in handfuls and put it between the logs of the house. She worked it in with her hands. The inside walls had already been done, and were covered with muslin flour sacks. Now the outside chinks must be filled, where the old filling had dried out and had been loosened by wind and rain.

Eva took up mud and began to help.

"This is hard work," she said. "Why can't Father and Andrew help?"

"It is no work for man or boy," said her mother. "They have not patience enough. Besides Father must look after the cattle and Andrew likes to ride the horses."

"So do I," said Eva, thinking of her pet pony, Queenie.

Soon she grew tired and sat down. She took little Joel in her lap and made mud pies for him.

"Come and help, daughter," her mother said. "If you want a warm house this winter, help me close the chinks to keep the cold winds out."

Eva worked until it grew dark. Then Mother went in to light the lamp and soon supper was ready. Father and the boys came back and they all sat down to eat.

THE ALARM CLOCK

One morning Eva woke up early. She heard the noise of chopping wood and jumped out of bed. She ran to the small window and looked out. There was Grandma Antelope in the snow, chopping wood. Grandma was always the first one up. Her bedding was already on the line by her cabin.

Winter had come now in earnest. The little town of Black Horse lay covered with snow.

The sky looked dark and heavy, as if it might snow all day. Eva heard a man's voice. There was Old Uncle Nick, standing outside his cabin, facing the sunrise, singing a Sioux song.

"What is he singing for?" Eva asked.

"For the soldiers who died in the war," said Mother. She took the alarm clock from a shelf on the wall. She shook it, but it did not start.

"Eva, you take the clock to teacher today," she said. "She fix it, so it keep time again. Tell her I'm out of lard and ask for some nails."

"Yes, mother," said Eva, pulling on her clothes.

Mother took little sticks of wood from a small pile and put them in the stove. The stove burned red hot and sent waves of heat through the chilly cabin.

Eva's two brothers, Andrew and Henry, rolled out of bed. They did not have far to roll, because their beds were blankets on the floor. They played with their dog Sparky.

"It's too hot in here!" said Andrew, puffing.

Steam from the kettle on the stove made white

clouds in the room. The kettle began to sing.

"Good thing we got all the cracks filled up tight," said Mother. "Now we have a warm house for winter."

"I like a tent better," said Eva.

"Uncle Nick lives in his tent all winter," said Andrew. "He never gets cold."

"He has two tents," said Mother, "one larger than the other, with air space between. That makes it warm inside."

"He has a camp stove on the ground, with no bottom under it," said Andrew. "When he makes a fire, it warms the ground all around."

"The old people say we were better off when we lived in tepees," said Mother. "In houses we all get sick. So much TB and all the kids get runny noses."

She picked up baby Joel, who began coughing.

The children took biscuits out of a pan on the stove and dipped them into the bowl of hot soup. The soup was jerked beef, cut in small pieces and cooked in salted water. This was their breakfast.

Clang, clang! The school bell rang. The boys

picked up their coats and ran out. Eva started to go, but Mother called her back and gave her the alarm clock.

Eva waded the snowdrifts, trying to catch up with her brothers. Other children were running out of other cabins. In spite of the cold, Anna Red Fish, the woman next door, was hanging clothes on her line. An old man stumbled past. Though buried deep in snow, Black Horse was coming to life.

The children ran across the snow-covered log bridge and up the slope on the other side. They passed Uncle Nick's white tent, which had a tin stovepipe coming out at the top. A wagon load of firewood stood beside it. Smoke was curling up from the chimneys of all the cabins. Some had willow shelters built at the side, the branches bare now and covered with snow.

"Wait for me! Wait for me!" called Eva.

But the boys were too far ahead to hear. Usually it took only five minutes to get to school, but today going was not easy. In some places the snowdrifts were so high, the children had to find

a way around them.

The school was a small white frame building with a row of six windows on one side. On a post in the yard hung the large iron school bell. Now it rang again, and the clanging sounds were carried away on the wind. The children saw Miss Watson, their teacher, outside pulling the rope. Then she hurried in at the door, her coat wrapped closely about her.

When Eva came inside, Miss Watson was not

at her desk. She was busy kneading dough on a table in the corner.

"What you do?" Eva asked, coming near.

"Oh, I'm baking bread again," said Miss Watson. "You children will be hungry today in this cold weather. It went down to zero last night."

"Zero—what's that?" said Tony Big Bear with a laugh. He opened his shirt and pounded on his bare chest. "I don't get no cold, I like it down to zero. I'm a big strong Indian, me!"

"Button your shirt, Tony," said the teacher, "and don't act silly."

"Miss Nan, our clock . . ." Eva set it down on the table, but Miss Watson did not look at it.

"Bring it to my house tonight, Eva," she said, "and I'll oil it for you."

"But we will come late to school, Miss Nan, if our clock does not go," said Eva.

"Do you forget to wind it?" asked Miss Nan.

Tony Big Bear picked up the clock and wound it tight. He held it to his ear. The loud ticking could be heard all over the room.

"Look! It goes!" said Tony. "I make magic! I make the clock go! No oil needed now."

Eva set the clock on her desk. Other children came straggling in. A heater stove for coal stood in the rear of the room, and beside it was a kerosene stove with an oven on top. The children took off their wraps and hung them in the entry. Then they watched Miss Nan put four loaves of bread in the oven to bake. They took their seats in three rows and settled down to work.

All morning the tiny room was filled with the delicious smell of fresh bread. After an hour the loaves, still warm, were spread on the table, upside down in their pans, cooling. And two pans of biscuits were put in to bake.

Everybody was hungry when the noon recess came. A large kettle of corn had been cooking on the stove. Each child came up with his dish and Miss Watson dished out his portion. They helped themselves to pieces of dry, crisp bacon. Then two of the girls passed the biscuits. After a short play outdoors, the afternoon passed quickly and it was time to go home. The children put their wraps on and ran.

Eva took the clock in her hands, but did not leave. Miss Watson banked the coal fire in the heater, put the room in order, then came out and locked the door. Eva walked behind her, stepping in her tracks. They came to Miss Watson's house beside the church.

Miss Watson was the only white woman in the village. She felt quite at home there, for she had taught at Black Horse School for eight years. She said good-bye to Eva, went in her house and closed the door behind her.

Eva waited a while, then went up to the door

and knocked. Miss Watson opened it.

"I came to visit you, Miss Nan," said Eva.

"But Tony wound your clock, Eva," said Miss Watson. "It will go all right now."

"I . . . er . . . well . . ."

"Now what, Eva?" asked Miss Nan.

"My mother . . ." began Eva.

"What does Mother want today?"

"My mother, she wants nails and lard."

Miss Watson was used to her neighbors' borrowing habits. Because they shared all they had with each other, she, too, must share with them. She brought a few nails in a sack and a small cup of lard. She gave them to Eva.

"Thank you, Miss Nan," said Eva.

"I'll see you at school on Monday, Eva."

"Good-bye, Miss Nan," said Eva.

The door closed and Eva started for home.

"PRAIRIE ROSE"

"Can't we go with you?" asked Eva. She held baby Joel in her arms.

"No," said Mother. "Father and I will be back tonight. Father got his government check, the lease money, so we go to town to spend it. You take care of the boys and baby Joel. If you need anything, go to Uncle Nick."

It was Saturday morning. John White Bird had his two horses hitched to the wagon. He and his wife sat in the front seat, ready to go.

"But, Mother," began Eva, "what if a big snow comes?"

"Keep the boys in if you can," said Mother.

"We must go to Watauga before the big storms come. We must buy food to last till spring."

Eva watched the wagon move slowly along the road and disappear over a hill. She hugged her little brother close. Now she must be Little Mother to Joel. The boys ran off with the dogs, but Eva went inside and closed the door. The cabin seemed quiet and empty without Mother. She could hear the alarm clock ticking loudly.

About noon it began to snow. Eva fed the boys when they came in. Then she sang the baby to sleep:

"Mother, oh come back,
Mother, oh come back,
Little brother calls as he
seeks thee, weeping.
Mother, oh come back,
Mother, oh come back."

Then Eva took pieces of cotton cloth and cut quilt patches for her mother. Mother's new quilt was almost done. It lay across the sewing machine in the corner, where Mother had been sewing. It was a pretty design. Mother called it the Rising Sun.

That afternoon the snow stopped, so Eva took

the baby in her arms and went out. She stopped
next door to visit Anna Red Fish. Anna's two
babies were playing with a kitten. Anna was
sitting on a canvas in the floor, plucking a porcupine. Eva watched her.

"Is it hard work?" she asked.

"Not very," said Anna. "It just takes time.
Some people in a hurry skin them, but they don't
taste good then."

Eva said, "Andrew and Tony Big Bear had
one in a barrel at school, but he got away.
Sparky, our dog, tried to catch him and got quills
in his nose."

Anna laughed. "This might be that very one.
I caught him down by the creek. They are not
hard to catch, they travel so slowly. You can run
up on one and hit him with a stick. I'll save the
quills to use for embroidery."

Eva did not stay long. She went next door to
the Black Arrow cabin. She wanted to see Sara,
her best friend. But no one was at home. Then
she stopped at Emma Grindstone's. Emma was
a large heavy woman. She had only one son and

he was sick. She had no little girls at all.

Today she was cross. "Don't come in," she told Eva. "Go away with your baby. Don't bring him in here. There is sickness in this cabin."

As Eva left, she saw Old Grandpa Many Deeds, the medicine man, coming along the path. She knew that meant that the Grindstone boy was very, very sick. The old man passed her, muttering to himself.

Eva went back to Anna Red Fish's cabin. Anna told her to let baby Joel stay and play with her own two babies.

"I'll go see Grandma Antelope," said Eva.

She hurried over to Grandma's cabin. Grandma's face was very brown and full of wrinkles. Grandma spoke only the Sioux language and never tried to say English words. So Eva spoke in Sioux, too. Grandma was beading a pair of moccasins. She was sewing with sinew, which she called *ta-honk*.

"Father and Mother went to town and left us," said Eva.

"You are big enough to stay home alone,"

said Grandma. "They will be back tonight."

"If there was a store in Black Horse," said Eva, "they would not have to go so far—all the way to Watauga. Is that a long way off?"

"Yes," said Grandma, "but they must buy food to eat."

Eva liked to complain to Grandma. Grandma was always sympathetic and took the children's part, especially if they had been scolded.

Today Grandma talked about her beadwork. She was one of the few Sioux women on the Standing Rock Reservation who knew how to make Sioux costumes from deerskin.

"The young women cannot make them," said Grandma. "They have not the patience, they have not the time. I tried to teach your mother when she was young, but it was no use. She had to go to school every day. Ah, times have changed, when a young woman no longer obeys her mother."

Eva watched Grandma's rough, knobby hands move gracefully, threading the tiny beads. She watched the pattern grow under her fingers.

Grandma told her the names of many designs—leaf, feather, arrow, forked tree and dragon fly.

"Who showed you how to do it, Grandma?" asked Eva.

"My great-grandmother and my grandmother," said Grandma Antelope. "They showed me how to cut and shape the deerskin. They taught me the meaning of each design, the number of feathers in a headdress, and other things."

Grandma looked Eva up and down.

"I could do pretty beadwork when I was younger than you," she said. "Now, a Sioux girl goes to school to a white teacher and learns how to read in a book. But the skills of her forefathers are forgotten."

"What did you make when you were a little girl, Grandma?" asked Eva.

Grandma's eyes lighted up. "Did I never show you?"

She went to her trunk in the corner, the trunk with silver buckles on the straps. She opened the cover, lifted something out and held it up.

"Oh!" gasped Eva. "A Sioux girl doll!"

It was a buckskin doll about ten inches high. The body was made of padded cloth. The fringed buckskin clothing was beaded in bright colors.

"I made it when I was six winters old," said Grandma. "I have kept it ever since. Now I will give it to you, my only granddaughter. Take care of it, Eva, give it to your own granddaughter when you are seventy-nine winters old like me. Do not lose it."

Eva took the doll and pressed it to her heart.

"I will always keep it," she said.

"Her name," said Grandma Antelope, "is *Blaye wagca*—Prairie Rose."

" 'Prairie Rose!' " repeated Eva, happily.

Chapter 2

A LONG WAIT

Eva loved her buckskin doll, Prairie Rose. She hid it away in the box where she kept her clothes. She slid the box under the iron bed where her parents slept. There were other boxes there, filled with washed and starched clothes, neatly folded. That night Eva fed the baby and gave the boys some supper, but she did not show them her doll.

It grew dark early and began to snow again.
Eva kept looking out of the window, hoping to
see a team and wagon drive up, but none came.

"When will Father and Mother get here?"
asked little Henry.

"Pretty soon," said Eva, hopefully.

But when she looked out the window, all she
could see was a blur of snow. Another blizzard
was coming. Would they be able to get home
tonight?

Again she sang the baby to sleep, *"Mother, oh
mother, come back . . ."* and her voice sounded
very sad. Andrew and Henry were tired from
playing out in the snow. She spread out their
blankets and they went quickly to sleep. Eva put
more wood on the fire and closed the dampers
of the stove. She looked at the small pile of wood
on the floor and shook her head.

"When Father gets back, he'll have to go out
and find wood," she said to herself.

She tried to wind the alarm clock, but it
would not go. Then she brought Prairie Rose
out from her hiding place. She took the doll in

her arms and held it close. It kept her from being homesick for Mother. Then she undressed, turned out the oil lamp and crawled into bed.

It was daylight when Eva awoke. The room was very cold for the fire had gone out. Eva got up quietly and made a fresh fire. Soon the boys were bouncing out of bed and playing with Sparky. Their noise woke baby Joel who was hungry. Eva cooked oatmeal for breakfast, but there was no milk or sugar.

"When are Father and Mother coming home?" asked Henry.

"I don't know," said Eva.

Andrew looked at the shelves.

"They better come quick," he said. "Not much left to eat."

Eva opened a sack.

"We've still got potatoes," she said, "and Miss Nan's lard."

It was Sunday, but the church bell never rang in bad weather. The priest could not come, so no services were held. It kept on snowing and blowing most of the day. Eva tried to keep the boys indoors, but they ran out. They did not stay long. It was no fun to play with the icy wind blowing in their faces.

That afternoon Eva put the last stick of wood in the stove. There was no use asking the boys to go out to get wood. The growing trees on the reservation could not be cut for fuel, so only dead or dry wood was used. And this would now be covered with snow.

"I'm getting cold," said little Henry.

The baby began to cry and cough fretfully. Eva quickly put on her coat and mittens.

"You come with me, Andrew," she said. "Mother told us if we need anything to go to Uncle Nick. Uncle Nick has a wagon load of wood."

Eva and Andrew hurried out, leaving Henry with baby Joel in his arms. Soon they came back, their arms full of wood. They stamped the snow off their boots before they came in.

"Now we will be warm again," said Eva.

"When is Mother coming back?" Henry kept asking.

"Not till it stops snowing," said Eva.

When it grew dark, Eva fried the potatoes in Miss Nan's lard for supper. She looked out of the window many times, but there was no sign of team or wagon. She knew now that her parents had probably not even left Watauga. Night came—the second night without Father and Mother. The little children went to sleep and Eva took Prairie Rose to bed with her.

When she awoke the next morning, it had stopped snowing. What time was it? The alarm clock had stopped at four-thirty. Was it four-thirty morning or evening? What day was it— Sunday or Monday? How many days had Father and Mother been away? Was this a school day or not?

"Did you hear the school bell, Andrew?" asked Eva.

"No," said Andrew. "If it rang, the wind blew the sound the other way." He cleared the frosted window, but could not see other children going to school.

After Eva and the boys were dressed, Eva

wrapped little Joel up, took him on her back.

"We'll take Joel to Grandma Antelope's first," said Eva, "before we go to school. You boys make a path for me."

It was hard going for the snow was deep. The boys went ahead and broke out a path, kicking with their boots. They went over the log bridge and up the other side. Soon they came to Grandma's house. Grandma lived alone, for Grandpa had been dead a long time. They all went in where it was warm and cozy.

"I'm hungry," said little Henry.

Grandma gave the children *wasna* to chew on. *Wasna* was jerked meat and dried chokecherries ground together. It was in a pan, cut in squares, and they ate it like candy. Grandma always kept *wasna* on hand.

"*Wasna* is good!" Andrew grinned. "When you eat it, you don't get hungry for a long time."

The children were so hungry, all they wanted to talk about was food. Henry said, "The meat I like best is prairie dog."

Andrew said, "I like all kinds of meat— beaver, porcupine, pheasant, grouse, partridge and skunk!"

Grandma laughed. She took baby Joel on her lap and fed him.

"More snow today," said Grandma. "The big storms are coming. Sit down and I will tell you a story—how the rainbow got its colors."

The children crowded round her to listen.

"One bright summer day," said Grandma, "all the flowers were nodding their heads in the breeze. There were red and yellow flowers, orange and blue and purple. The Great Spirit heard them talking together.

" 'I wonder where we will go when winter

comes and we all have to die,' said a little red flower.

" 'It doesn't seem fair,' said a blue one. 'We do our share to make the earth a beautiful place to live in.'

" 'I think we should have a happy hunting ground of our own,' said a little yellow flower.

"The Great Spirit thought so too, and decided they should not die when winter came. And now, so the Sioux legend says, after a refreshing shower, all the bright-colored flowers are seen in the rainbow, as it makes a beautiful arc across the sky."

The children smiled, for they loved Grandma's story, but they had to go. "You keep Joel today?" asked Eva. Grandma nodded yes.

"You don't stay long," said Grandma. "Why you rush off?"

"We got to go to school," said Eva.

They ran out. When they reached the school-house, Eva remembered something. "Grandma never asked us if Mother and Father came back."

"No," said Andrew. "She thought they were

at home. She thought they got home Saturday night the way they said they would."

A DAY AT SCHOOL

When Eva and the boys came in, they saw they were late. The other children were all in their seats. Miss Watson was serving the hot lunch.

"Why . . . are we late?" gasped Eva.

"Late!" said Miss Watson. "Where was your alarm clock? Didn't you hear the school bell? It's noon. You and your brothers have been absent all morning."

Eva sat down and buried her face in her hands. She did not like to be scolded by Miss Nan. How could she know what time it was? Sara Black Arrow brought Eva's lunch and set it on her desk. Eva was so hungry, she dried her tears and ate.

Suddenly a loud roaring noise was heard. It sounded like the roar of a motor. Every one looked up.

"I hear an airplane, teacher!" said Tony Big Bear.

"Yes, Tony," said Miss Nan. "Now read the next paragraph aloud to us."

"But, Miss Nan, it's flying *low!*" cried Tony.

Tony was a boy who could not see anything inside his book, but who never missed seeing everything outside it.

"Eva, will you please read?" asked Miss Nan.

Eva stood up and began.

But Tony interrupted. "He flew low, Miss Nan! Something fell off the plane! It hit the church steeple. I saw it!"

All the children jumped up and ran to the

windows. There was nothing Miss Watson could do about it. They saw several Indian men wade through snowdrifts over to the church. But the airplane had not landed. It had flown away into the dark clouds.

The children went back to their work again.

An hour later, a man came to the schoolhouse door. It was Luke Fire Cloud. He brought a letter, a newspaper and several magazines for Miss Watson.

"Mail!" cried Miss Nan. "I thought I would not get any mail until spring! How did the mail get here? After a big storm like this. I thought the road would be closed for weeks!"

Luke Fire Cloud spoke rapidly in the Sioux language. Tony Big Bear interpreted.

"I was right!" said Tony. "The airplane brought it! The pilot threw down a bag of mail and hit the church steeple with it!"

The children giggled and laughed.

"Luke Fire Cloud say it's the *air lift!* The *air lift!* The pilot he been throwing out hay for the cattle to eat, to keep them from starving. The pilot brought groceries, too, from McIntosh. Enough for the whole town of Black Horse to eat! They're over at Luke Fire Cloud's house!"

Tony pretended to gobble imaginary food and the children laughed.

"A grocery store at Black Horse!" laughed Andrew.

"My mother and father didn't need to go to town, after all," said Eva. "But they never knew the *air lift* was coming."

Miss Watson heard her. "Why—when did they go?" she asked.

"On Saturday," said Eva.

"When did they get back?" asked Miss Nan.

"Not yet," said Eva.

"They're not back yet?" asked Miss Watson. "Why, today's Monday! Why didn't you tell me? Have you been staying alone?"

"No," said Eva. "I had Andrew and Henry and Joel."

"You little children . . . all alone through that storm?" asked Miss Watson. "Did you have any breakfast?"

"We had *wasna!*" Little Henry grinned. "It was good."

"When will they come back, Miss Nan?" asked Eva.

Miss Watson looked worried.

"Not till the road is opened," she said.

HOME AGAIN

But the children did not have too long to wait. They spent another night alone and another day at school. Then they came home and ate the supper which Miss Watson had given them in a pail. While they were eating, they heard noises outside.

"Here they are!" cried Eva.

She and the boys went out to welcome the wagon. Sparky came too, barking noisily.

It was Tuesday night when John White Bird and his wife, Ramona, returned to Black Horse. They had been stranded in Watauga all day Sunday. Early Monday they started out and it took them all day to get to McIntosh, ten miles. And all day Tuesday to go the eighteen miles from McIntosh to Black Horse. Father had to dig the wagon out of the drifts many times.

How happy the children were to see their parents again! Father brought the groceries in and Mother put them on the shelves. The children helped to carry the paper bags. There was a lot of everything—potatoes, flour, lard, sugar, canned milk, macaroni, baking powder, coffee, onions, matches, canned meat, canned tomatoes and peaches.

"Now we eat good again!" said Andrew.

When the food was unpacked, Father took the team and went away to get a load of wood for fuel. He would have to dig for it under the snow.

Eva told Mother all that had happened.

"Why didn't you tell Anna Red Fish that you were alone?" asked Mother. "She would have helped you."

"She had her own babies to take care of," said Eva.

"Why didn't you tell Grandma Antelope?" asked Mother.

"You told us to go to Uncle Nick if we needed anything," said Eva. "Andrew and I went over and he gave us wood. So we had a warm house."

"Good!" said Mother.

"We went to Grandma's," said Eva, "but she thought you got home on Saturday. See what she gave me." She showed Mother the Sioux Indian doll.

Mother was pleased.

"You must take good care of Prairie Rose," she said. "I loved her too, when I was a little girl like you."

Chapter 3

MOVING DAY

Winter was over and spring had come to the little village of Black Horse. The meadow larks were singing and the prairie grass was turning green. On the last day of school, Eva brought Miss Watson a bouquet of wild pasque flowers which she had picked on the hill above the creek.

46

Miss Watson thought they were beautiful.

A day or two later, the three White Bird children came to the teacher's house. Eva knocked at the door and Miss Watson opened it.

"We have come to visit you, Miss Nan," said Eva.

"Come in, children," said Miss Watson.

They went inside. They held their arms folded around their waists. Their jackets bulged in front.

"You are hiding something in your Indian pockets," said Miss Watson, laughing. "What have you got?"

Each boy drew a little white puppy out from under his jacket.

"Puppies!" cried Henry.

"Our dog Sparky had puppies last week," said Andrew. "Their names are Rocky and Rascal."

Miss Watson patted the puppies on the head.

"And I have a doll," said Eva, opening her jacket. "Grandma Antelope made her long ago. Her name is Prairie Rose."

"What a beautiful doll!" said Miss Watson.

"We are going home now," said Eva. "Good-bye."

Miss Watson saw the family wagon, piled high with belongings.

"Oh, to your river home, you mean," she said. "Do you like it there?"

"It's nice in summer," said Eva, "big trees and water."

"Good-bye," said Miss Watson. "Have a happy summer. I'll see you again in the fall."

The children ran out and climbed in the wagon, where John White Bird and his wife waited. Sparky, the dog, scampered about, barking. The teacher went back in her little white house and the wagon went off down the road.

Most of the Black Horse cabins were empty now. The Indian families were moving away to their river bottom homes. Father had moved the stove, the sewing machine and the big armchair the day before. Now they were going to stay all summer and Eva was glad.

They had about eleven miles to go. Eva knew every inch of the way—every boulder and rock and bush and hill and cliff. She knew every little creek that drained into the Grand River. Father did not follow any road. There were no roads over the grassy prairie slopes. The horses seemed to know just where to go. They kept up a steady pace. Eva wondered when she would see Queenie. The ponies were turned loose to forage for themselves.

Father drove by George Barber's place and stopped. George Barber was a white rancher, who rented reservation land from John White Bird. George was a good friend and neighbor.

Mr. Barber was in the barnyard. He had a ruddy face and a friendly smile. He came to the wagon and talked.

"I went up to Fort Yates last week," he said. "Went up to the Agency to pay for my lease."

"Good!" said John White Bird. "I always get my checks on time."

"I passed Nicholas One Elk on my way back," said Mr. Barber. "Brought him home in my pickup. He had walked all the way up there and was starting back."

"Uncle Nick—he likes to walk," said John White Bird.

"It's a long way to Fort Yates and back," said Barber, "and he's getting old."

"Old age don't stop Uncle Nick," said John White Bird. "He's seen ninety-six winters on these prairies."

Eva saw the Barber children over beyond the barn. While the men talked, she and Andrew ran over to see what they were doing.

"Hi, Eva!" called Lily Barber, a girl of eight.

"Hello," said Eva, shyly. "What you doin'?"

Lily's brother, Mark, had dug a hole in the ground. He picked up a dead animal and threw it in the hole. Lily held her nose shut. The air was filled with skunk odor.

"Did you kill a skunk?" asked Andrew.

"My father did," said Mark.

"Why did he kill it?" asked Andrew.

"It's been killing our chickens," said Mark. "We heard a terrible row in the night. Our dogs barked and barked. My daddy came out and found this mean old skunk in the chicken house, and shot it."

"What did he kill it for?" asked Andrew.

"I told you—it was after our chickens." Mark shoveled dirt on the dead animal.

"Grandma Antelope says . . ." began Eva.

"You don't *need* it?" asked Andrew.

"Need it?" Mark laughed. "What would I need a skunk for? It's good for nothing."

"It good for many things," said Andrew.

"Grandma says, keep it for oil," Eva ex-

plained. "It's good medicine, for rheumatism. Just warm the fat and rub it over the spot where it aches."

The white children laughed.

Lily Barber said, "Do you believe that, Eva?"

"Yes," said Eva. "My grandma say so."

How hard it was to make white children understand things!

"It's no good to us," said Mark Barber, tramping the dirt over the hole.

John White Bird called and the children ran back to the wagon. They drove on, waving their hands to the white children. All the rest of the way, Eva kept thinking about the skunk.

Soon they came to lower land, where trees were growing along Grand River. Fresh green leaves were budding out in the spring sunshine. There were no trees at all at Black Horse or near it. It was good to see trees again. The wagon passed one or two Indian cabins. The children saw other Indian families moving in. They saw some grazing ponies, but Queenie was not with them.

Down in the low places water was standing

and it was muddy. The wagon had to pass through mud holes and the gumbo mud was sticky like gum. It stuck to the wagon wheels and did not fall off. It rolled up like a snowball. The wheels got muddier and muddier, until the horses could not pull the wagon.

Father had to stop before the wheels became mud-locked. Father and Andrew took sticks and cleaned the mud off the wheels. In one hole, the wagon got stuck. Father and Mother and Eva and Andrew all got out and pushed. Eva saw a gumbo lily blooming. She picked it and then they went on again.

At last they came to their own cabin. It stood on a little mound beside a creek that ran into the river. And there was Eva's pet pony, Queenie, waiting for her! Yesterday Father had hobbled her so she could graze near camp, and he could use her in rounding up the other ponies and cattle.

Father stopped the horses by the door and they all jumped out. Sparky and the two puppies pranced and barked. Eva ran over and put her arms around Queenie's neck. She untied the pony's feet, jumped on her back and went galloping off, her hair flying in the wind. Soon she came back.

"At home again!" she cried.

She ran in at the open door.

HIGH WATER

It was good to be in the river bottom again, until it began to rain.

Father said, "The frost is out of the ground. The river is getting higher. Maybe there will be a flood."

"We are safe," said Mother. "The river never came up this high before. Stay and eat supper."

"No, I must go," said Father. "I must get my cattle out of the lowlands. I must save my cattle feed."

Father rode off in the rain on one of the horses, and the children did not see him for two more days.

"Is there going to be a flood?" asked little Henry.

"In the spring, the river is always high," said Mother.

That night Mother and the children went to bed early. Toward morning, Eva was wakened by the barking of a dog. She heard Mother call to Sparky to hush. Then it was quiet again, except for the sound of the pouring rain. It rained as if it would never stop. Then Eva was awakened again, this time by a man's voice.

"Sleeping is nice," the man said, "but when you are in danger, it is better to wake up."

Mother answered, "But the river never came up here before."

"It is here now," said the man. "Come and help others, if you do not want to help yourself."

"Last year nobody helped us," Mother grumbled. But she was already up and had the coffee pot on the stove. "I will make them some coffee!" she called out.

It was getting daylight by this time. Eva jumped out of bed and pointed. "The water is coming in under the door! Look!"

Andrew and Henry got up and stared. Baby

Joel began to cry.

By this time, Mother was wide awake. Alarm showed on her face.

"Quick!" she cried. "We must save things! We can't let everything be washed away!"

"What shall I take?" cried Eva, standing helpless.

Andrew wasted no time. He picked up the armchair and carried it out. He came back for the sewing machine. Eva helped him, while Mother rolled up the bedding.

"Shall we put everything *out in the rain?*" cried Eva.

Mother put baby Joel in Eva's arms.

"Where are we going?" asked Eva, wide-eyed.

"I don't know," said Mother. "They'll take us somewhere."

Mother rolled all the bedding up in a big roll, her quilts inside. The roll was all she could carry. She put it outside the door in the rain. She ran back to put pans and dishes in a basket.

"Take the food, Andrew," she said.

The boy took the sack of flour out. Eva, still

holding the baby, picked up the lamp. Just then
a team of horses, pulling a wagon, stopped by
the door. It was Nathan Thunderbird again.

"Leave your things, Ramona," he called.
"Save yourselves. When you see the river rolling,
that is no time to think of worldly goods. Come,
we have room for you and your children. Get in."

Other people were in the wagon, Anna Red
Fish and her babies and the Fire Cloud children.
Mother and Eva and the baby and the boys
climbed in, too. It was still raining hard.

"But my armchair?" cried Mother. "My bedding, my sewing machine, my quilts? Who will save them for me? Are they then to be left out in the rain, to be carried away by the river?"

"This is no time to think of sewing machines," said Nathan Thunderbird. "Human lives are in danger."

He whipped up the horses and drove through water to higher land. Once the wagon hit a floating barrel, which broke the doubletree. Nathan stopped to fix it, using a wire he took from his pocket. They drove on and came at last to a stopping place.

Other wagons and several cars were on a hill. A bus driver was sounding the horn of his bus to urge people to leave their homes by the river. A dam had broken and water would soon be in all the cabins.

Many Black Horse people were on the hill. Tents were already up and fires made to keep the people dry. Eva and Alice Fire Cloud and Sara Black Arrow took care of their little brothers and sisters. Alice's little brother Tommy had saved his pet kitten from the flood.

Tommy showed it to the other children. It was black with white paws.

"Her name is Black Spider," said Tommy. "See, she got white *hands!*"

The girls laughed.

Indian bread was passed and everybody ate. All day long, the children played in one of the tents. Before night, Father returned and said he had saved some of the cattle. He brought his tent and set it up. Other tents were provided for other families.

"Must we then sleep on the wet ground?" asked Mrs. White Bird. "How can we sleep without bedding? Nathan Thunderbird left ours behind."

Blankets and quilts were given to the White Birds and, tired out, they went to bed.

The next morning, the sun was shining brightly, and it was easy to forget the dangers of the day before. Eva heard the women talking.

"So Ramona saved her armchair and lost her bedding," said Mrs. White Tail. "I saw them dump her chair off a wagon. She now has a big chair to sit in, but no bed to sleep in."

"Yes," said Mrs. Fire Cloud. "The White Birds got out in time, but left their bedding behind."

The women laughed.

"Who would be so foolish as to forget bedding!" said Mrs. White Tail.

"Anybody would," said Mrs. Black Arrow, "when her life is in danger."

"That Ramona!" said Mrs. Fire Cloud. "You should hear her grumbling! And well she might, for it was nice bedding, too. She's a great one to make patchwork quilts. And she lost her new one, the Rising Sun!"

Just then Nathan Thunderbird walked by.

"This will teach you women a lesson—to get out of the river bottom," he said.

The women looked at the man and tossed their heads.

"But it's so beautiful in summer down here," said Mrs. Black Arrow.

"And all the chokecherries and juneberries we

want!" added Mrs. Fire Cloud.

Eva's mother joined them.

"When can we move back into our cabins?" she asked.

LITTLE DOLL LOST

"Let me sleep in the tent all summer, Mother," begged Eva. "It's nicer than the cabin."

The tent had been moved down beside the cabin and it was to be the family sleeping room.

When the river went down, a sea of mud was left behind. Mrs. White Bird and Eva carried water from the creek. They scrubbed the cabin inside and out. They moved the furniture back in. They had new bedding now, given by friends and neighbors.

Father and the boys cleaned up outdoors. Many logs and broken trees had been carried by high water and left on the land. Father and Andrew chopped the logs and piled the wood in piles.

Father cut green willow branches and built a *wikiup* at the side of the cabin for shade. He put branches on the east and west sides, and also over the top. He made a rough table and benches. The Indians called the wikiup a "squaw shade," because the women liked to sit there to keep cool on hot days.

One morning, Eva went out to hang the bedding on the line. She heard some one chopping wood and it made her think of Grandma Antelope. Then suddenly, she remembered the little buckskin doll. Where was Prairie Rose?

Eva ran into the cabin and opened the boxes where Mother kept their clothing, but the doll was not there. Mother was busy at her sewing machine, sewing patches together to make a new quilt.

"Have you seen my doll?" Eva asked.

"Why, no," said Mother. "Where did you leave it?"

"I don't know," said Eva. "I haven't seen it for a long time."

"Did you look in the boxes?" asked Mother.

"Yes, but she's not there," said Eva. "What will Grandma say if I've lost Prairie Rose?"

"Don't worry," said Mother. "You'll find her, I'm sure."

Eva looked inside and outside of the cabin, but the doll was not there. She tried to think when she had last had it—not since they had left Black Horse. She remembered taking it with her to show to Miss Watson. She had held it on her lap as they rode away from Black Horse in the wagon. Or, had she? She was not sure.

Did it fall out of the wagon on the way to the

river bottom? Did she take it to bed with her the night before the flood? She could not remember. Maybe she dropped it at Miss Nan's and never had it on the wagon ride at all. She could not be sure. All she knew was that it was gone.

Mother called her to come and help plant garden. Mother made the rows and told Eva to drop the seeds. Corn, beans, squash, pumpkins, melons and cucumbers were to be planted.

Eva picked up a sack of shelled corn and began to drop it.

"Not there!" called Mother. "Beans go there. The corn will go down in that low part. Are you dreaming, daughter? Don't you hear what I say?"

Eva started to drop beans in the row. But her row was very crooked.

"Go away, daughter," said Mother. "You don't know how to plant garden. Andrew! Where's Andrew?"

But Andrew did not come.

The tears came to Eva's eyes. She did not like to be scolded. She went off and sat down on a rock. All she could think of was her doll. Where was Prairie Rose?

The next morning there was great excitement around the White Bird cabin. George Barber, the rancher, had lost two of his cattle in the flood. He sent word to John White Bird that he would pay him for skinning them. Mr. Barber would keep the hides and the Indian women could have the meat.

John White Bird brought the beef home in his wagon. The neighbor women came to take care of the meat. They worked at the table in the *wikiup* beside the cabin. They talked and gossiped as they worked.

"Is it true that Emma Grindstone's boy has TB?" asked Mrs. Big Bear. "Is that why she stays at Black Horse all summer?"

"Yes, it is true. Poor boy—he is so sick!" Mrs. Black Arrow shook her head. "If she came down here and lived in a tent, he might get well."

"Maybe they will take him to the sanitorium in Rapid City," said Mrs. White Tail.

"Oh no!" said Mrs. Black Arrow. "He would

only die there, so far from home. Better to call in Grandpa Many Deeds. Better to use his medicine that comes from the ground."

"If it is TB," said Mrs. Big Bear, "then there is no hope."

Eva stood by the table and listened. She watched Mrs. Big Bear make jerked beef. The woman took a knife and whetted it razor sharp on a smooth rock. Then she spread the muscles out into long, thin, narrow strips and hung them over poles in the direct sunlight to dry. The pieces were paper thin and of irregular shape, spread apart with slender twigs. All the women helped. Eva cut a few pieces and spread them thin.

Eva grew tired and walked away. She saw Andrew on his pony, Red Winter Baby. She ran, jumped on Queenie's back and caught up with him. Andrew had to ride out and count the cattle daily, to see that none had strayed away or gotten mixed up with other cattle. Eva had ridden a horse ever since she was a baby and her father had lifted her up to ride in front of him.

Out on the range, galloping in and out of the bushes, she forgot her sadness and was happy again. The sun felt good on her back and she liked the wind blowing through her loose hair. Once when they stopped, she saw a bank of wild roses in bloom—lovely wild roses that grow nowhere more beautiful than on the prairie.

Prairie Rose! The thought of the buckskin doll came back again. Where could she be?

Chapter 4

BERRY PICKING

"Come, children," called Mrs. White Bird. "Today we will go berry picking!"

"Hooray!" shouted Andrew. "Berry picking is fun!" Eva was excited, too.

"The June berries are ripe," said Mother. "We must get all we can. When they are dried and pounded, I will put them in flour sacks and hang them up for winter."

"Make *wasna!*" cried Andrew. "Make *wojapi!*"

"The chokecherries will be ripe in July," said Mother. "Dried June berries and chokecherries together, with flour and sugar, that makes good *wojapi* to eat in winter time."

"Yum, yum!" said Andrew. "I like pudding —*wojapi!* We will pick bushels of berries, so you make plenty *wojapi!*"

Soon they started out, Andrew and Henry,

Eva, and Mother with baby Joel in her arms. They all carried baskets and pails. They followed a well-worn path over the lower ground to the higher slopes. Here bushes and trees grew thick on the east side of a butte.

It was a beautiful summer day, not too hot. A gentle breeze was blowing. It rustled the leaves on the trees and waved the high grasses.

They had not gone far when Andrew said, "I hear people talking."

"Everybody will be out picking berries today," said Mother. "No one could stay at home on a day like this."

It was true. The Big Bear and the Black Arrow families were already out. Mrs. Big Bear came up, carrying two large pails filled to the top.

Mrs. White Bird stared in surprise.

"Such big ones, Arlene!" she cried. "Where did you find them?"

Arlene Big Bear tossed her head. "Over there," she said, waving her hand in the air.

Mrs. Big Bear and her children, all with pails

full, passed on, taking their berries home. Only
Tony stopped to play with Andrew. Soon the two
boys were wrestling on the ground. When Andrew gave Tony a hard punch in the stomach,
Tony howled and went running after his mother.

Then the Black Arrow family came up. They
had just come out, and their baskets were empty.

"We will go together," said Mrs. Black Arrow to Mrs. White Bird. "There are enough berries for all."

Eva was glad to see Sara Black Arrow and her
little sister, Winona. Sara was her best friend.
Sara's hair was as straight as Eva's, but every
night she put it up in curlers, trying to make it
curl. Eva took Sara's arm and they whispered
together.

"Eva!" called Mother. "You girls get those
berries off that big bush there, while we pick
these low ones."

The June berries grew on low bushy trees.
They looked a little like blueberries, but the berries were so dark when ripe, they were nearly
black.

Soon everybody was picking busily. The berries thumped on the bottoms of the tin pails until they were covered. Mother put baby Joel down on the ground to play with little Henry. The women talked as the picking continued. Picking berries was a slow and tiresome job, but the Indians were never in a hurry.

Suddenly a sharp cry rang out, and everybody stopped to look.

"Oh! Oh! Oh!" cried Eva. "I'm stung, I'm stung!"

Dropping her pail, she turned and ran. Sara ran, too, and Winona after her.

"Bees! Wasps! Hornets! They're after me!" cried Eva.

Sara turned back, pointing. "See that hornet nest—right there in that little tree where we were picking! They're all after us—the hornets!"

"I'm stung! I'm stung!" cried Eva, weeping. "They've stung me a dozen times!"

"Come here, Eva," called Mother. "Let me see."

The girls came back and every one crowded round. It was true—Eva had a big sting on the side of her cheek. It was swelling rapidly and looked very red.

"You're only stung once," said Mother.

Mother went to a wet spot, mixed some mud with water and put wet mud on the sting. She covered it with a green leaf.

"It will stop hurting soon," said Mother. "You can stop crying."

But Eva sat down on the ground and cried for a long time. Andrew called her a baby, but she cried all the more. Eva had a soft heart and she liked sympathy. But no one paid any attention to her.

"Shall we knock it down, Mother?" asked Andrew, pointing to the hornet's nest.

Tony Big Bear was back. He came up now with a heavy stick. He swung it back and forth, ready to hit the nest. Mrs. White Bird caught his arm just in time. She threw the stick to the ground.

"No, Tony!" she said sternly. "Let the hornets alone. They have a right to live, too, just as we do. They only sting us if we disturb them. Let them alone. Come, we will find our June berries somewhere else."

Tony went off grumbling.

Soon Eva got tired of crying and looked up. They had all gone away and left her, even Sara, her best friend. There was the hornet's nest still hanging in the June berry bush, with the hornets buzzing around it. It was so large, she wondered how she had failed to see it. And there at her feet was her pail and all the berries she had spilled.

Eva was glad to be alone.

The others could all go off and leave her if they wanted to. Let them pick berries all day. Who cared? Pick, pick, pick all day long. There was no fun in that.

Eva got up and walked. She wandered through briars and bushes. She found some buffalo berries, growing on a little bushy tree. She tasted them, but they were not ripe yet. The Indians liked to eat them raw, but did not pick them until after frost. Sometimes they sold them to white people for jelly. They were pretty to play with even when green. Eva picked some and put them in her pail. She decided to string them for a necklace when she got home.

She walked along slowly. Once she pulled some wild onions and ate them. They were getting too strong now. When the first green shoots came up in the spring—that was when they were tender and delicious. She knelt down and munched quietly. Then she saw something. A little runway through the grass led to a nest on the ground arched over with dry grass for a roof.

A meadow lark sat on the nest, so close Eva could almost touch it. She saw the stripes on its head and its bright eye looking at her.

The next minute it was gone. Up in the sky it flew, its glorious song floating behind, filling the prairie with the sound of Sioux words. In the nest were five white eggs with small reddish-brown spots. She did not touch them. Suddenly a little rabbit hopped out beside her. She sat very still and watched it. Its nose kept twitching and its bright eyes looked into hers.

At that moment, she felt at one with all living things. But only for a moment. The rabbit turned and with a flip of its white tail, was gone. Eva laughed aloud. Then she heard a rustle in the bushes beyond. Was it one of the ponies? She turned just in time to see a large buck deer with a small spotted doe at his side. Eva's heart skipped a beat. Then, sensing alarm, they bounded away and she was left alone.

She got up and walking on, saw some Indian turnips. They had silvery leaves and furry stems, with little flowers of deep blue veiled by fuzz.

They were hard to dig by hand, but Mother liked them. She peeled the black leathery coating off the roots, sliced and dried them, then cooked them with meat in the winter time. The Indians had many uses for the leaves, roots, fruits and berries of plants that grew on the prairies.

Eva thought of Grandpa Many Deeds, the medicine man. He gathered sweet grass, wild sage, cedar tree needles and all kinds of roots. He said all plants were given to people to use for food and medicine. The Black Horse people did not like doctors, although the Indian Agency paid their bills. Whenever any one was sick, the medicine man was called in. Grandma Antelope made her own medicine. She had never been to a doctor in her life.

Suddenly Eva remembered Prairie Rose, the little buckskin doll that Grandma had made and given to her. Where was Prairie Rose? How could she have lost her?

When she got back to the cabin, the others were there before her. Mother had the June berries picked over and was getting ready to dry them. She spread them out on papers in the sun. The baby was crying and Eva had to change and comfort him. Then it was time to eat.

PLAYING HOUSE

One day the girls went down to the river bank to play. Besides Eva and Sara, there was Sara's little sister, Winona, and Alice Fire Cloud. They wore home-made bloomers and waded. They splashed and threw water on each other. They swam for a while, then came back out and sat on the bank. They put their dresses on again.

Then who should come but Mamie White Tail! Mamie was older than Eva and Sara, and they did not like her much.

Mamie said, "Let's make chewing gum!"

"Chewing gum!" said Eva. "You buy that at the store in town."

"I don't mean that kind," said Mamie.

She took a knife from her pocket and cut some bark from a tree, which had glassy leaves and gummy sap. She beat the bark with a heavy stone and washed away the fiber in the river. The girls watched in surprise. Then Mamie chewed the gum that was left. She said it tasted good.

"Give us some, Mamie!" begged Eva.

"Is it really good?" asked Sara.

Mamie gave them some gum to chew. She gave some to Winona and Alice too. The gum had a sweet and pungent flavor.

"It's good, Mamie," said Sara. "Who told you about it?"

"Grandpa Many Deeds," said Mamie. "He knows everything. He's never been to school a day in his life, and yet he knows everything."

"Let's play house," said Sara. "Let's build a tepee and go visiting."

Sara and Winona had brought a bundle of old cloth and blankets with them. They opened the bundle and brought out their dolls. They had some rag dolls made from old socks and some small rubber and plastic dolls from the dime store in town.

Sara always had ideas and liked to pretend. She told the others what to do. They gathered dead branches and Mamie cut poles for the tepees with her knife. Alice Fire Cloud helped her.

"Tepee! Who knows how to make a tepee?" asked Mamie.

"I do," said Eva. "I watched Luke Fire Cloud make one, once when we went to Fort Yates to a rodeo on the Fourth of July."

Eva showed the girls how to set the poles up in a circle.

"It takes twenty poles to make a tepee," she said.

"You want me to cut twenty poles?" asked Mamie.

"Sure," said Eva. "I'll help you."

They soon got tired of cutting poles, and decided ten would do. When the poles were cut, they set them in a circle and tied them together at the top. They cut more poles for a second tepee and set it up.

"I'll cover mine with deerskin," said Eva, picking up a piece of cloth.

"I'll use a big, big buffalo hide for mine," said Sara. She picked up a blanket.

"It takes twenty deerskins to cover a tepee—one for each pole," said Eva.

"But my hide is from a giant buffalo," said Sara. "Don't you remember when the men went to the Black Hills to find meat and brought back that big one? It was a fifteen hundred pound bull buffalo they had for that feast for Black Eagle's son. Its hide was half as large as our schoolroom. Miss Nan didn't know that buffaloes grew so big!"

When the two play-tepees were finished, the girls played house, visiting from one tepee to another, imitating their mothers. The tepees were just large enough to crawl into.

"Your tepee is crooked!" said Mamie White Tail, laughing at Eva. "It will fall over when the wind blows."

"No, that is the right way to make it," said Eva. "Longer on one side than on the other. Luke Fire Cloud said so."

Mamie made a *travois,* by fastening two long poles together with ropes. Alice was the horse to pull it. Sara put her bundle and her little sister on it. Sara tied all her dolls on a stick and put a shawl around her shoulders. She went to visit Eva in the other tepee.

"Here I come with all my children to stay a week," said Sara. "How are you, Mrs. Rain-in-the-Face? Where are your children? How many have you got now?"

"None," said Eva, sadly. "My children are dead. I buried them in the cemetery. I made paper flowers all winter to put on their graves."

"But they didn't all die," said Sara, who called

herself Mrs. White Lightning. "Where is your baby? Her name was Prairie Rose."

"I lost her," said Mrs. Rain-in-the-Face. "We went on a long journey, over a long, long trail, and when we got there, we found we had lost her. She must have been left behind."

"Did you go back and look for her?" asked Sara.

"No, I forgot!" said Eva. Then, looking up, she said suddenly, "But I will! Why didn't I go before?" She jumped up and ran out of the make-believe tepee.

"Come back!" cried Sara. "You can't go off like that." She pointed to the opening in front of Eva's tepee. "You can't leave your door open. Anyone could break in. The evil spirits might come . . ."

"That's right," said Eva. "I will lock the door."

She covered the opening with canvas and pushed an old box up close. She crossed two poles in front.

"Now everybody will know there is no one at

home," said Eva. "No one will enter. Good-bye!"

Sara, Winona, Alice and Mamie thought she was still pretending. "Good-bye!" they said.

But Eva did not wait to finish the game. She ran up the slope as fast as she could. Once when she came to higher ground, she turned and looked back. The other girls were staring after her. Then she was gone.

THE SEARCH

Eva walked slowly. If only she could ride Queenie! But no, the pony galloped so fast, she could never look closely. She would have to walk. She followed an old buffalo trail over the rolling prairie. It was hard to believe what the old people said, that great herds of buffalo once roamed where she walked. There were no trees at all, except those along the creek. The top of the Barber ranch house could be seen over the brow of a hill. Back and beyond was a view of Grand River and rocky buttes.

But Eva did not notice the landscape. She kept

her eyes fixed on the ground. If she had dropped the buckskin doll from the wagon that day, she knew she would surely find her. Very few people crossed the prairie except in wagons—cars kept to the graded roads. No one would have picked the doll up. Even though it was small, the color of the buckskin was light and she would be sure to see it.

Eva remembered that Father had driven into the Barber barnyard. He always stopped there when passing by. George Barber was his adopted "brother." The two boys grew up together and were lifelong friends.

When Eva came closer, she saw that the Barber yard was full of children. Boys, girls and dogs were running and playing and making noise. The Barbers must have company, for several cars were parked by the fence. The children were having a wonderful time, but Eva could not see Lily or Mark anywhere.

Eva was shy and afraid to go in. If she did, the children would all stop their play and look at her. They would ask her what she wanted and she would not be able to tell. If she said she was looking for a doll, they would laugh at her. If she could only see Lily outside somewhere, alone. Then she would not be afraid. She would ask her if she had found the doll.

Eva hid behind a board fence and watched the children. They were playing "Andy Over" around the summer kitchen. Half the children were on one side and half on the other. When one side threw the ball over the roof, they called out, *"Andy OVER—R—R!"* If one of those on the other side caught it, he ran back to tag someone on the other side. This made a grand scramble and was fun.

Eva forgot she was hiding. All the Indian children loved games with balls, and Eva was no exception. She sat up on the gate to watch better.

Then one of the children saw her and pointed.

"Oh, look!" she cried out. "There's an Indian watching us!"

A boy shouted, "Give me my bow-'n'-arrow, I'll put a shot through her heart!" He pretended to shoot Eva.

Before she could climb down, all the children had crowded round her. They all had white faces with light-colored eyes and hair. They all pointed and grinned at her.

"Where'd you come from?" "Where do you live?" "At Little Eagle?" "Bullhead?" "What you doin' here?" "Nobody asked you to come." "Gonna steal something?"

Eva could not bear it. Her heart began to beat very fast and she trembled. She hid her face and cried. As she climbed down from the gate, she

stumbled. She fell to the ground and lay there.

The children stopped teasing and became quiet. A woman called from the back door. Dinner was ready and they ran away and left her. Eva started to get up.

Then she felt an arm around her shoulder. Through her tears, she saw that it was Lily—little Lily, whose hair was the color of sunshine. Lily's blue eyes looked red now, for she was crying, too.

"I'm sorry," Lily said. "They didn't mean to hurt you. They just don't know any better. Don't cry, Eva, I love you."

Eva dried her eyes and felt better.

"Where's your wagon?" asked Lily. "I didn't see it come in."

"It's not here," said Eva. "I walked."

"You walked?" said Lily. "Why, that's a long way from Black Horse."

"We're in the river bottom now," said Eva.

"Are you going somewhere?" asked Lily.

Eva managed to say something about her doll, but Lily did not seem to understand.

"Your doll?" said Lily. "I never knew you

had one. Do you love dolls like me?"

Eva nodded. "Did you find it?" she asked.

"No," said Lily. "I never saw it. I never knew you had one."

That was all Eva wanted to know.

"I'll go now," she said.

"Come back again," said Lily, "any time."

Chapter 5

EMPTY VILLAGE

It was a long way from the Barber ranch to Black Horse, but Eva walked it. She felt she had to go there before she went back home. She thought of Grandma Antelope first. But Grandma was not there, she knew that. In the summer, Grandma stayed at Uncle Jerome's up

the river. Besides, Eva did not want to see her. She could not tell her she had lost the buckskin doll.

What a strange Black Horse it was! All the cabins were empty and deserted now. A high wind swept across the plateau, blowing a cloud of dust and sand in her face. It was not a pleasant welcome.

Eva had never been at Black Horse in the summer before. It all looked strange and different. She went over to the school and looked in the window. There were the three rows of seats, the stove and the teacher's desk. There on the blackboard was the drawing of a horse. Eva smiled. Tony Big Bear liked to draw horses better than to study his books.

Sadly Eva turned away. She passed the church and peeped in the window of Miss Watson's house. Where was Miss Nan? Why did she go far away in the summer and leave her little Indian friends?

Eva crossed the footbridge over the creek. Even the cabins looked different. She did not try

any of the doors, though she knew they were un-
locked. Some had two crossed sticks in front, a
sign that no one was at home. They were all
empty inside.

All? Was that a wisp of smoke coming out of
the last chimney? Or was it only a cloud?

Eva came to her own home, the White Bird
cabin. Dust and tumbleweeds were banked
against the wall. The wikiup at the side was bare
of leaves and branches. The cabin was no longer
inviting—it was no longer "home."

She opened the door and went in. Still thinking
of the lost buckskin doll, she looked around inside. Rags and papers lay on the floor, with some
empty cartons. She looked carefully, but there
was no sign of the doll.

She came out again, and placed the two
crossed sticks before the door. Everybody was
gone, all the Black Horse people . . . All? Eva
wondered. Looking closely at the sandy ground,
she saw footprints. They were not from store-
bought shoes with a hard heel, but from soft Indian moccasins. Whose could they be? There

was no one in sight. The prints were fresh. Some one must be near.

Out by a pile of trash, Eva saw an empty oil can and a rag that had been dropped. It had oil on it, it smelled of harness oil. She went on and came to the creek. She looked closely. Somebody had been tanning hides. She could see where the bundle of hides had been soaked in the creek and dragged out.

Tanning hides was a tedious job that lasted a week or longer. Some one had scraped the hair off with a bone scraper. It was a deerskin—the pile of loose hair looked reddish in color. They had greased it here with harness oil from the can. They had pounded yucca root for soap, and spread the grease and soap over the hide to soften it. Then they had soaked it for several more days in the creek.

But if they did that, where was it now? It must be stretched out, drying somewhere. Maybe Grandma Antelope had been here, working up deerskins for new moccasins.

Eva walked around and came to Grandma Antelope's house. It was deserted, too, like all the rest. But Eva's eyes were sharp. There was the post where Grandma pulled the hides back and forth to soften them. She looked at the ground and saw moccasin footprints around the post. Perhaps they were Grandma Antelope's. Eva's heart gave a great lift! Grandma had been here! Grandma wasn't far away. Where had she gone?

Then Eva grew sad again. If she found Grandma, how could she bear to tell her she had lost the doll?

Where was Grandma now? And when was she coming back? Eva sat in the doorway of Grandma's cabin and waited. Surely Grandma would come. She wanted to tell Grandma everything. Only Grandma could help her. She could not go home till Grandma came.

The afternoon sun that had shone so brightly, began to get lower now. It sank farther and farther down in the west as Eva watched. The great dome of the sky had never looked so vast, and the horizon so far away before. The evenings were long on the prairie—it was a long time be-

fore bedtime. Surely Grandma would come.
Grandma would make a bed for her and she
could sleep in Grandma's cabin.

But when darkness came, a lonely little girl
was still curled up in the cabin doorway, fast
asleep.

TRIP TO TOWN

"Well, look who's here!"

Eva heard the words and looked up. It was
morning and she was still lying on Grandma An-

telope's doorstep. Emma Grindstone and her husband, Alonzo, were looking down at her.

"Eva White Bird!" cried Emma, in surprise. "What are you doing here? When did you come?"

"I came to see Grandma Antelope," said Eva, "but she was gone."

"She was here last week, tanning a hide," said Emma. "She came again yesterday to get some of her things, but she didn't stay."

"Where did she go?" asked Eva. "Back to Little Eagle?"

"Your Uncle Jerome brought her in his car," said Emma. "She came to get her billfolds and belts and moccasins. Uncle Jerome took her to the Indian Agency at Fort Yates to sell them."

"Oh!" said Eva. "That's why she didn't come back."

Emma Grindstone was a woman of few words. She asked no more questions about why Eva was so far away from her river home.

"My boy is sick," said Emma. "We took him to Rapid City and left him there. I came back and have been picking chokecherries to sell in town." She pointed to her husband's car and said, "Come, get in. We'll go now."

Emma got in the front seat beside her husband. The back was filled with pails and baskets of chokecherries. Eva made a place for herself, climbed in and sat down. She had not had many automobile rides and was afraid. She held her hand on the door, ready to open it and jump if necessary.

The road that connected Black Horse with the rest of the world was rough and full of ruts. It had been a trail once, then a wagon trace, and now, though sometimes used by automobiles, was not graded or paved. It wandered in and out among rocks and boulders, and up and down over dried-up hollows, steep slopes and wind-swept heights.

The Grindstone car, a rickety secondhand one, shook and trembled, but kept on going. Eroded cliffs loomed up and deep gullies sloped down into stagnant water holes. There was no tree, no grass and hardly a bush. Now and then a cow or sheep was seen, looking for grass.

Eva knew that this road went to town. Not to one town but to all of them. It was the way out— to stores and movies and rodeos and trading centers. Those who left Black Horse must always travel this rugged path.

For not only did the rugged rocks and cliffs make the road itself hard to travel, but rains turned its mud holes into pools of danger, and snows in winter made its steep slopes hazardous with ice. Like many wiser people at Black Horse

than she, Eva wondered if she had not made a mistake to come.

At first she thought that the Grindstones would take her to the Barber ranch and leave her. But they went past the trail that turned off to the right. They went past the White Shirt School, as deserted now as the one at Black Horse. Were they going to McIntosh, or to Watauga or Walker— all those towns that were equally dreamlike in Eva's mind?

They did not tell her. So Eva sat back in her seat, helpless. There was nothing she could do.

Suddenly the Bad Lands vanished. The road became smoother, the hills less rough. The Grindstone car came into a town—what town Eva did not know. She saw houses and yards with fences, and feeble trees trying to grow. Then she saw stores and sidewalks, and people walking by. Soon the car stopped, and with the Grindstones, she climbed out.

"You hungry, Eva?" asked Emma.

Eva did not know how hungry she was until the food was set before her. The restaurant had several people in it, eating at small tables, but no one looked her way. Eva ate what Emma Grindstone ordered for her, and it tasted good. After that, Emma took her pails and baskets and went off to sell her cherries. Eva waited on the sidewalk near the car.

Once she walked down to the biggest store of all and looked in the window. There, with a lot of other toys, she saw a doll—a large life-size store doll with curly hair and eyes that opened and shut. It had on a pink flowered dress that stood out on all sides. Eva looked and looked. It was a feast for her hungry eyes.

Then some one called her name. To her surprise, she looked up and saw Lily—white-faced Lily with the golden hair. It was her friend, Lily Barber. Lily was in town, too, with her family. Lily said she came once a week and sometimes twice, to go to "the show." But Lily saw that Eva was not listening. Lily saw that Eva's eyes were glued to the pretty doll.

"You like that doll, Eva?" asked Lily softly.

Eva had no words for the longing in her heart.

Dumbly, she nodded yes. Yes, I like it. But not half as much as I liked Prairie Rose who is lost and gone forever. But this she could not say to Lily.

"Do you like it *very, very* much?" asked Lily. Lily's eyes were bright with a secret she could hardly hide.

Eva nodded.

"You wait here," said Lily, "till I see my mama and daddy. Wait here—don't go away."

Again Eva nodded. Then Lily was gone.

And before she knew it, Emma Grindstone held her arm in a tight grip, and Emma Grindstone was pulling her toward her car.

She tried to protest, "Lily told me to wait . . ."

Lily? Lily who? Emma Grindstone had no patience with an unknown Lily. It was time to go. Emma was tired and cross—she had not sold half her cherries. They were already late. They would have to go a long way off the Black Horse road to take Eva to her river home.

"I should not have brought you along from Black Horse," said Emma, grumbling. "I should have made you walk back the way you came. And now, because of you, we've got to ride half the night on that dark and tricky trail—just to take you home . . ."

Eva curled up in the back seat and said nothing. But her heart was very heavy.

SAFE AND SOUND

"Hello! Hello! Anybody home?"

When the Grindstones reached the White Bird

cabin in the lowlands, it was the middle of the night. It took a lot of shouting to wake up Eva's family.

Eva's mother came out at last, with a flashlight in her hand.

"How can you sleep so soundly," asked Alonzo Grindstone, "when one of your children is lost? Have you then no heart?"

"So there she is!" Mother said, with a laugh. "Safe and sound. To think of all the tears I wasted! We could not find her all over the river bottom. We looked for two days and a night. I felt sure the river had claimed her. The other girls said she went swimming . . . there is a bad current around that bend . . ."

"So you come home and sleep soundly," said Alonzo Grindstone. "I must shout loud enough to waken the dead to get you up!"

Eva stood still and hung her head, listening to the grownup's angry words. No one asked her to tell where she had been. No one wanted to know her side of the story.

Eva's father came out.

"My daughter was not lost, I knew it," said John White Bird. "She is a girl of good sense. I told Ramona to go to her bed and sleep. I knew some neighbor, some kind neighbor like Alonzo Grindstone, was taking care of her."

"Yes ... yes ... I was," said Alonzo. "I did the best I could."

But Emma Grindstone was not so meek.

"All on account of your daughter, John White Bird, we had to drive thirty miles out of our way in the darkness of the night . . ."

"Good, good!" said John White Bird. "I will shake your hands. You are neighbors worth having. Wait, I have something for you."

He went indoors and came out with a sack of flour. He put it in the Grindstone car. Then there was much shaking of hands. The two women shook hands, and the two men did the same. The White Birds shook the hands of the Grindstones over and over again.

"Good night, our good neighbors," they said. "Come again soon." That ended the matter.

Mother and Father did not ask Eva where she

had been. Eva was back, Eva was well and happy. No harm had come to her. What more could they ask?

Down on the river bank the next day, Eva played house again with Sara and her sister Winona. They brought a bundle of scraps and began sewing doll clothes. To Eva, their rag and rubber dolls were poor and shabby things, after the beautiful doll in the store window in town. She wondered how they could love them so much.

Then with a pang, she thought of Prairie Rose, and in her heart, she knew. Remembering the wild roses blooming on the prairie, she made up a little song:

> Little wild rose growing on the prairie,
>   Turn your face to the sun.
> Little prairie rose, when the winds blow,
>   Turn your face to the sun.
> Little prairie rose, when the storms come,
>   Hide away under the snow,
>   Sleep, sleep well
>   under the snow.

Chapter 6

LITTLE SIOUX GIRL

Eva did not want to go.

Even though Mother said they must, even though it was September and school would soon re-open, even though she would see Miss Nan again, Eva did not want to go back to Black Horse.

To her, as to all the Indians, the cabin in the lowlands was her real home. She loved the grass, the trees and bushes, the river. She loved the outdoor life she lived there. And somehow, now, the spirit of Prairie Rose, the little buckskin doll, haunted the place. She did not want to go.

"Take these things and put them in the wagon," said Mother.

Eva picked up the pans and kettles and put them on the load. She carried out bundles and boxes of clothing. Then she swept the cabin floor for the last time.

Mother and Eva went out to the garden. The beans and cucumbers were all gone, but squash, pumpkins and corn remained. Father and the boys were gathering the corn. Eva helped pick the pumpkins and squash and take them to the wagon. These vegetables would be dried for winter use.

Then the White Bird family climbed up in their places. All but Andrew, who was to come behind on his pony, Red Winter Baby, with sacks of corn behind him. Eva said good-bye to

Queenie and turned her loose to roam and forage for herself on the range.

To Eva, the ride was a long farewell. It was good-bye to the June berry bush with the hornet's nest, good-bye to the bush where she saw the deer, good-bye to a hundred summer memories, good-bye till another summer would come. Each turn of the wagon wheels took her farther from the scenes she loved so much. Each turn of the wheels took her closer to Black Horse, to school and to the long hard winter.

Could she love village life again, with close neighbors who knew everything she did and heard everything she said? Could she love the crowded life with never a minute to think alone? Could she go back to her desk in school and sit all day long—she who was happiest when bouncing on the back of her pony, at one with the sun and the breeze? Could she be happy cooped up all winter in over-heated buildings, cut off from green growing plants, from animals and birds?

Eva said no word all the long slow way back. Her heart was very heavy.

Then they were there. The horses crossed the dry creek bed and stopped beside the White Bird cabin. The crossed sticks were gone from before the door. It stood open—an invitation. Father had brought a wagon load the day before. Inside was the meager but familiar furniture—stove, table, rolls of bedding—those things that made it home. Gone was the bleakness of that sad day in summer, when Eva had looked at emptiness. Now the house was alive again with people. Mother and the children, Father—it was people who made a building a home.

Black Horse the village, too, was alive. All the Indian families had returned. Black Horse was no longer empty cabins, dust and tumbleweed. Black Horse was laughter, loud voices, dogs barking, babies crying, the smell of good food cooking, smiles on neighbors' faces.

Suddenly Eva's sadness left her. It was good to be home again.

One day Grandma Antelope came walking in. She was glad to see Eva and asked why she had not come to visit her. Eva hung her head in shame.

Grandma took her by the hand. "Come, my granddaughter," she said. "Come, I have something to show you."

Would Grandma ask about the lost doll? No, she did not mention it. Grandma had other things on her mind.

It was good to visit Grandma again. Grandma had her trunk open, and her old Sioux Indian costumes spread out on her bed. She showed them to Eva and told her about them. She had one man's and two women's costumes, besides belts, arm bands and purses, all made from the finest deerskin, all richly beaded and decorated.

"There are few Sioux costumes left any more," said Grandma. "My people have sold them, given them away or been cheated out of them."

She took out a very special one to show to Eva. It was a small size, made for a little girl. It was very pretty, with handsome designs in beads and porcupine quills.

"This is what I wore when I was your age,"

said Grandma Antelope. "But before I put it on you, I must braid your hair in two braids."

After Eva's hair was braided, she put on the costume piece by piece. First she put on the beaded leggings, tying the thongs below her kneecaps, and the moccasins. Then she put on the ankle-length skirt and the cape with flowing sleeves. Last of all she put on the heavy necklace or breastplate, which was made of bone hair pipes, with a fringe of nickel-plated disks.

"Now you are truly a little Sioux girl!" said Grandma.

Eva was very excited. When she looked in the

mirror, she hardly knew herself. She went out of the house and ran from cabin to cabin. She showed everybody in Black Horse her Sioux Indian costume. The old people smiled happily to see her. The mothers said she looked nice. But the other children just laughed. Some even teased her.

"What you want to be an Indian for?" they jeered. "Why not be an American?"

"The Indians were the first Americans, Miss Nan said so," replied Eva. "I am a Sioux and I am an American. I will be both!" She spoke with pride, remembering the words of her grandmother and her school teacher. Both of them were right, she was sure of that.

In spite of the teasing, Eva wore her Sioux Indian costume to school. She wanted to show it to Miss Watson.

Miss Nan told her it was beautiful. She told her to always be proud of her Indian heritage. She asked the children to sing a song in the Sioux language and they did. She asked them to dance a Sioux dance. There was not much room between the rows of seats, but they did the best they could.

Miss Watson asked the children to tell her some Sioux words. This they did with much giggling. She asked Eva to dance. Eva danced a toeing-in dance in the aisle. The children giggled and made Eva feel badly. She put her head down on her desk for a long time. Then Sara, her best friend, came over and whispered something in Eva's ear that made her smile again.

When Miss Watson asked for a boy's dance, Tony Big Bear spoke to the others. Five boys got up and shuffled about. Then they stopped, laughing. The dance was over.

"That was the shortest Indian dance I ever saw," said Miss Watson.

"I like to make horses better than dance," said Tony.

He took a wire out of his pocket and bent it in the shape of a horse's head. He tied a red string to it for a bridle.

"My horse War Paint!" said Tony, holding it up.   The children laughed.

ANDREW'S SLED

"Is winter coming so soon?" asked Eva.

"Yes," said Mother. "We must get ready for it."

After the first frost, the White Birds made a trip back to the river bottom to gather wild grapes. The grapes had a sweeter taste after the frost had nipped them, Mother said. Eva loved picking and soon had her pails full. She helped Henry fill his, while Andrew went after buffalo-berries, which were ripe now, too. The small red berries were not only good to eat but good for jelly. Andrew chopped off the branches and beat them on a canvas, to knock the berries off. When they got home, Mother put them in a tub of water, causing leaves and twigs to float on the top, to be skimmed off by hand. Father traded the buffalo-berries to Mrs. Barber for making jelly, and took chickens in exchange.

After the first fall of snow, Eva and Andrew went for a walk over the prairie, tracking field mice to their holes. The holes were full of wild beans which had been carried there by the mice for their winter food supply.

"We need them more than you do, mousie," said Eva, scooping the beans out and putting them in her pail. "But we won't let you go hungry. We'll give you corn to eat, instead."

Andrew took shelled corn from the sack he carried. The children filled the mouse hole, and went on to find another.

"Yum, yum!" said Andrew. "Now we eat good this winter. Me—I can just smell these beans cooking."

"Ground beans are good," said Eva, remembering.

The first heavy snow brought out all the sleds in Black Horse. They were a mixed lot. Most were homemade, some were store-bought, while those of the little children were cardboard cartons. Most of the sliding was done on the hill south of the schoolhouse, so the children did not have far to go.

Andrew took his iron sled, of which he was very proud. He had worked hard for a whole week on Mr. Barber's ranch, helping with the haying in late summer. When he left, Mr. Barber gave him the sled. It was not new, but an old one that had belonged to Mark. Mr. Barber had bought Mark a larger and better one.

Mark's old sled was as precious to Andrew as his pony, Red Winter Baby. This was the first good snow on which to try it. He brought it out and was soon zooming down the hill.

Then Tony Big Bear came, noisy, blustering, troublesome Tony.

"Let me ride your sled," begged Tony, who had no sled of his own.

"No, you'll break it," said Andrew.

"I won't," said Tony. "You let me ride it or I'll . . ."

Soon the two boys were fighting, rolling over in the snow. Tony gave Andrew a hard blow and he did not get up right away. Then Tony ran off with Andrew's sled.

By the time Andrew got up, Tony was gone. He was running to a pond, where the water was frozen over. He started sliding on the ice. All the children followed and stood on the bank.

"Don't go there! Don't go there!" called Eva. "The ice is not safe. Nathan Thunderbird told us the ice is not safe."

But Tony did not listen. Down on the sled he flopped, while the sled moved fast. A crack was heard. The next minute the ice gave way, and boy and sled slipped into the cold black water.

The children on the bank began to scream. A man up by the cabins heard them and started running toward the pond. But Andrew was there already. He had to think quickly. What could he do? If he could find a board, he could pull Tony and the sled out.

He looked and saw a post, where an old fence had fallen down. He ran to it and tried to pull it out of the frozen ground. Suddenly it broke off. He picked it up and ran with it to the pond.

By this time, Nathan Thunderbird was there. He shouted loud words in the Sioux language. But that did not stop him from action. He grabbed the post from Andrew's hands, crossed the ice part way, laid the post down, then crawled out on it to reach the boy.

Eva and the children held their breath. Could he save Tony? Even though Tony, bad old Tony, was so often full of mischief, they did not want him to drown.

In a few minutes, the boy was dragged from the water, cold and dripping wet. Nathan Thunderbird slung him over his shoulder like a bag of meal, and hurried with him back to the village.

Andrew and the children followed close at his heels. Andrew cried out in dismay, "But Uncle

Nathan, my sled . . . my sled . . ."

Nathan Thunderbird turned and spoke in a stern voice. "A human life is more important than a sled," he said.

It was enough.

Andrew gulped back the tears and said no more. He would never mention the lost sled again.

Eva came up and took Andrew's hand in hers.

"I lost something once," she said. "I know how it feels."

But Andrew jerked his hand away.

For days afterward, he spoke no word.

NEW YEAR'S FEAST

"Can I wear it again, Grandma?"

"Once more," said Grandma Antelope. "You can wear it to the New Year's feast. Then I put it back in the trunk to keep it safe."

Eva could hardly wait for the day to come. For Christmas, several mission boxes had arrived, and the other children received new clothing,

which they would wear. But Eva looked forward
to wearing the little Sioux girl costume.

Winter was late this year. There had been no
heavy snows, so everybody was able to come. The
Indian women spent days preparing the food
and gifts. A calf, given by one of the men, had
been butchered and the meat was roasted, boiled
and made into soup the day before.

The feast was to be held in the Meeting House,
a special log cabin provided for social affairs.
Long tables along both sides of the building
were covered with freshly-ironed white table
cloths. Some of the cooking was done in the
homes, but most of it was done on the big iron
stove in the corner.

New Year's Eve came at last and the party began.

When Eva came in, everybody looked at her.
It made her shy. She hid behind her mother's
skirt. She would not look up or answer questions.

Andrew and Henry ran about with their
friends. The dogs, Sparky, Rocky and Rascal,
dashed about with the children and other dogs.

Tony Big Bear was there, showing off. He wore cowhide pants with fringes up the side, a bright-colored shirt and a leather jacket. On his head, he sported a large war-bonnet, full of feathers. He danced and cavorted, making everybody laugh. "A big strong Indian—me!" he kept saying.

Then it was time to eat.

Eva sat down on a bench beside her mother and tried to hide. Plates piled high with food were passed. There was plenty to eat. The meal began with meat. Potatoes and fried bread were passed. There was *tipsla,* Indian turnips served in a kind of soup. There were several kinds of pie and cake, besides cranberries and pickles.

It was hard for Eva to eat, with the heavy clothing weighing her down.

"Mother, I'm too hot," she said. "Can I take the costume off?"

"No, no," said Mother. "You wanted to wear it, now you must keep it on."

"I ate too much," said Eva, pressing her stomach.

There was too much food, it was true.

Mother had a pail, and she was putting left overs in it to take home. The Indians, who so often knew hunger, never allowed food to go to waste. Other women were doing the same. They wrapped up the more solid food to take it home to eat later. The whole village would eat well for a week after the New Year's feast.

Then came the speeches. Nathan Thunderbird was master of ceremonies. He introduced the speakers one by one. Nicholas One Elk, the oldest man in the village, spoke first. He was followed by several others, and by an interpreter who repeated in English what they had said.

After the speeches, which were very long, the exchange of gifts began.

Each donor had a friend speak for him. Joe Fire Cloud promised money for next year's feast. He made the gift in memory of his father-in-law, who had died a few months before. Many people went over and shook his hand. Dora Spotted Horse, speaking for her sister Clara, promised five chickens. James Shooting Bear promised five bales of hay to Roy Black Arrow. Roy shook hands with James. Carl Takes-a-Gun gave gifts of tobacco to all the men present. There was more shaking of hands.

The children waited patiently to hear their names called. Who would be first? They began to grow impatient.

Eva whispered to Sara Black Arrow, "I hope my name is not called," she said. "I'll die if I have to go up in front. Oh, why did Grandma let me wear this costume?"

"Don't worry," said Sara. "They all think you look pretty in it. They all like you for wearing it. None of the rest of us has a Sioux girl's costume to wear."

It was Sara's little sister, Winona, who was called first.

Nathan Thunderbird shouted, "Little Miss Winona Black Arrow will shake hands with little Tommy Fire Cloud for a kitten!"

"*Haw!*" answered the crowd, meaning, *Yes!* The people clapped and stamped their feet.

Winona and Tommy walked to the front of

the room. Winona shook hands with Tommy and received her gift of a kitten. Now, for Tommy to give up Spider, his black kitten with "white hands," was almost like giving up part of himself, since the Indian children loved their pets so much. But this was the Sioux custom. Unless the gift was something you treasured yourself, unless the gift was a sacrifice, it was not a gift at all. The Sioux people made themselves poor, giving gifts they could ill afford.

No more children were called for a while. Towels, blankets, aprons, pillow tops and cotton print for dresses were exchanged by the women. The children grew restless and tired.

Eva's costume was heavy and uncomfortable. She went over to her mother. She wanted to go home to bed. Just then her name was called.

"Eva White Bird will shake hands with Mamie White Tail for a . . ."

Eva was so astonished, she did not hear what she was to get. She was overcome by fright and could not move, until Sara and Alice pushed her forward.

"Go!" they urged. "Go and get it!"

Mamie White Tail! What could Mamie give
her? Eva could only think of the chewing gum
Mamie had made out of the bark of the tree down
by the river. The next thing Eva knew she was
up in front, shaking hands with Mamie White
Tail. Mamie was smiling broadly. Mamie was
handing out a gift.

Then Eva saw it—it was the lost buckskin doll,
Prairie Rose. Eva trembled so when she saw it,
she nearly let it fall.

"Haw! Yes!" cried the people, laughing and clapping. "The little Sioux girl! The little Sioux girl!"

As Eva stumbled back to her seat, many of the women stopped her. They shook her hand and looked pleased.

"A little Sioux girl for sure!" they said. "The doll matches your costume! Your Grandma Antelope is a fine woman."

Eva held the doll close, the doll she had never expected to see again. But Mamie White Tail —what was Mamie White Tail doing with Prairie Rose? Eva could not understand. As soon as the gift giving and hand shaking were over, Eva hurried to her mother's side.

Mrs. White Bird was looking at a quilt, held up by three other women—Mrs. Black Arrow, Mrs. Fire Cloud and Mrs. White Tail.

"Why yes, it certainly *is* my quilt," said Eva's mother. "I called it the Rising Sun. That blue is from my sister's dress, that red I got from the mission box . . ." She turned to Mrs. White Tail and spoke crossly. "How is it you give me my *own* quilt for a gift and expect me to shake hands with you?"

Mrs. Black Arrow and Mrs. Fire Cloud also looked at Mrs. White Tail, waiting for her to explain.

"After the flood this spring," Mrs. White Tail began, "the men on the hill gave us a bed roll and this quilt was in it. I did not know it was yours."

Mrs. White Bird looked puzzled. "I put my bed roll outside my door that morning," she said, "but I never saw it again. The river was coming in at the door. The river washed it away."

But Mrs. Black Arrow laughed. "Oh, Ramona, don't you see? It is easy to understand. Those men, who took us out in wagons, they took your bed roll up the hill after they took you! They saved it for you!"

"And I thought the high water carried it away!" said Mrs. White Bird, relieved.

"Then," added Mrs. Fire Cloud, "they gave it to the White Tail family to sleep on that night, and they kept it! Don't you see?"

"Trust the men to mix things up," said Mrs.

Black Arrow.

Mrs. White Bird reached over and shook Mrs. White Tail's hand.

"Thank you for keeping it for me, neighbor," she said, "and for giving it back as a gift."

"I meant it for a gift," said Mrs. White Tail, "not knowing it was yours already."

Then Eva spoke up.

"Mother, look what Mamie gave me," she said. "My doll, Prairie Rose."

"Your *doll!* It was not lost, then?" asked Mother.

Mrs. White Tail laughed. "The doll was in the bed roll! My girl Mamie—she's too old for dolls, she will soon be a woman. She heard your girl say she had lost a doll, so Mamie wanted to give her one!"

The women all laughed again. Grandma Antelope came and everything was explained to her. Grandma laughed with the others.

But Eva only smiled, as she hugged Prairie Rose to her heart.

Hearing singing, she looked around. The end

of the old year had come and the end of the feast, and the song was *Till We Meet Again*. Part of the people marched around, shaking hands with those still seated. Many eyes were wet and tears streamed down the faces of those who had lost dear ones during the old year.

Then they all got up to go. The feast was over. They walked back to their cabins with the words of the song ringing in their ears, *God be with you till we meet again!*

THE END